Counting Back from Nine

Counting Back from Nine

Valerie Sherrard

Fitzhenry & Whiteside

Published in Canada by Fitzhenry & Whiteside, 195 Allstate Parkway, Markham, Ontario L3R 4T8

Published in the United States by Fitzhenry & Whiteside, 311 Washington Street, Brighton, Massachusetts 02135

www.fitzhenry.ca   godwit@fitzhenry.ca

10 9 8 7 6 5 4 3 2 1

Library and Archives Canada Cataloguing in Publication
Sherrard, Valerie
    Counting back from nine / Valerie Sherrard.
ISBN 978-1-55455-245-0
    I. Title.
PS8587.H3867C68 2012   jC813'.6   C2012-904073-8

Publisher Cataloging-in-Publication Data (U.S.)
Sherrard, Valerie.
    Counting back from nine / Valerie Sherrard.
[200] p. : cm.
Summary: A high-schooler comes to terms with the loss of her friends and the revelation of family secrets that cause her to question everything she thought was true about her life in this free verse novel.
ISBN: 978-1-55455-245-0 (pbk.)
1. Coming of age—Juvenile fiction. 2. Friendship in adolescence—Juvenile fiction. 2. Teenage girls—Juvenile fiction. I. Title.
[Fic] dc23   PZ7.S54773Co 2012

ONTARIO ARTS COUNCIL
CONSEIL DES ARTS DE L'ONTARIO

Canada Council
for the Arts

Conseil des Arts
du Canada

Cover and interior design by Daniel Choi
Cover art by Francesco Paonessa
Cover images courtesy of Jaime Reid and Michelle Bagley, and Shutterstock
Printed in Canada by Friesens in October 2012

Job# 78305

The author gratefully acknowledges the support of the Canada Council for the Arts which last year invested $24.3 million in writing and publishing throughout Canada.

L'auteur remercie le Conseil des arts du Canada de son soutien. L'an dernier, le Conseil a investi 24,3 millions de dollars dans les lettres et l'édition à travers le Canada.

Acknowledgements

My editor, Christie Harkin, signed this story as prose, which is how it was first written. When I sent her a note proposing a complete re-write in free verse, I expected, at the very least, some hesitation. Instead, the suggestion was met with enthusiasm and support. I don't know how often an author is given that sort of go-ahead on a contracted story, but I suspect it's relatively rare. For that, and for the fine editorial guidance she provided, I am most appreciative. Thank you, Christie!

My friend Marina Cohen read the earliest version of this story, gave me terrific feedback and often kept me going with her enthusiasm. Thank you, Marina!

My friend Marsha Skrypuch read a free verse draft and offered invaluable suggestions, which solved several problems, and may have prevented a breakdown. Thank you, Marsha!

My husband, Brent, listened ever-so-patiently to a *lot* of whining during my struggles with *both* versions of this story. He's kind of a saint. I kind of love him. Thank you, honey.

Secrets

When IT began I thought I would
crumble, fall apart, blurt it out. Confess
everything. Or get [caught]. That was the
worst thought of all.

Guilt and fear whispered in me until they
had me convinced I was sending out signals
(((((((i)))))))
But no one noticed a thing.
My friends trust me.

We're at Angie's place at the moment.
The four of us. Me—Laren (rhymes with Karen)
Morgan, Angie and Nina.
It's pouring rain outside, but we don't care.
We've got movies and snacks.
We've got the house to ourselves.

I'm about as relaxed as I've been since IT began
until Morgan says, oh-so-casually,
"I don't know who you think you're fooling about Scott.
Everybody knows what's going on."

My insides turn to jelly,
heat shoots up my neck and spreads over my face
while I search frantically for   something   anything
to say
some way to explain.

The room has gone as silent as death.
I lift my chin, forcing myself to face Morgan,
only to find her
stone-faced and staring at
Nina.

"Seriously, Nina. We don't want to be mean,
but it's been nearly two months
Two months, Nina!
since you and Scott broke up. You have to let go.
You haven't even changed your Facebook status.
There's nothing "complicated" about
being single.

Nina fights back through her tears.
"It's not that easy. I love him.
I have to see this through to the end."

"The end already *happened*," Morgan says.
She's right.
And no one in the room
knows it better than
I do.

So here I am,
watching
silently hoping they win this war
and my betrayal reaches full circle.

I need to get out of there.

I mumble an excuse.
Another lie on the heap.

Reflections on Cause and Cure

I'm not quite sure how this works but   Scott
seems to be the remedy, the thing that
chases off my guilt about   Scott.

My status tells anyone who cares
that I'm single.
The truth is: in my case, it really *is*
oh so complicated.
The worse I feel about all the lies,
the more I want to see and touch   Scott,
to press my face against his chest
and breathe. Just breathe.

His voice on the phone sends a thrill
skittering through me.
"I want to come over. Okay?'" One thing about   Scott:
he never wastes time getting to the point.
No discussion, no middle ground. It's yes or no.
I hesitate, calculating the risk of discovery,
until his voice shifts into low gear.
"I'm on my way, Laren. I have to see you."
And my heart smiles.
Well, if you *have* to   Scott.

Introductions

Too late, I realize I haven't warned Scott
to look Mom in the eye when he meets her.
Her Mother Brain positively rattles with crazy truisms.
This is one of them.
"You cannot trust a person
who won't look you in the eye," she says.
Because there couldn't *possibly* be any other reason
for a person not eyeballing you.
Like shyness or nervousness.

I see her making a mental note to discuss it with me later.
She'll say:
"I'm not judging." And I'll know right away that she means
Scott.
"I want to give him the benefit of the doubt.
I just can't get past the feeling that
this boy isn't quite
trustworthy."
At some point, she'll drag out the word
'shifty'

but at least that will be later.
I tell her that we're going to listen to music in my room.

So, naturally, her Mother Brain
makes her yell down the hall after us:
"Just make sure you keep the door open!"
I'm mortified, but he laughs it off,
pulling me tight against him,
smiling into my eyes,
kissing me until my head swims
and all that exists is
Scott.

Discovery

How could I have fallen asleep?
There we were, lying side by side ... talking
while strains of Coldplay cushioned the empty spaces.
At first I think he's gone but when I turn, he's sitting
on the side of the bed, looking bored.
He feels me stir. He tells me he's got to go.
All the tenderness has drained out of him.
I say I'm sorry—I don't know what
happened—I'm so sorry.

"It's not that, Laren. It's *this*.
We can't *go* anywhere or *do* anything."

Tongue-tied, I follow him to the front door

And then Fate smirks and steps in,
planting Angie at the end of my driveway.
I don't see her until I've kissed him goodbye.
I don't see her until my eyes follow Scott leaving
and find her standing there.
Still as a stone.

Unanswered Angie

Shame silences me and so
I do not say
anything.

But she is right.
I cannot expect her to
keep this quiet
and
I should have the
decency
to tell Nina myself.

Mostly True Confession

There's no right way to tell
this kind of thing to a friend. So,
I get it over with quick and
move on to dressing the wound.

I'm so sorry. Really. Truly.
I never meant for this to happen.
I hope you can forgive me.
Please, forgive me.

Her answer is back in a flash. The speed of light.
The speed of anger.
I'm ready for a huge blast but it's short and to the point.

I hate you.

Sinking In

She can't really hate me.
Not after all the years we've been friends.
Not over one thing. One guy.

This is turnabout. Fair play.
A stab in my heart
to repay
the knife in her back.

I know what's next and I don't have long to wait for
Morgan's monologue.

> I can't believe you kept this from me!
> How do you think *I* felt hearing it from *Nina*?
> Sometimes it's like I don't even *know* you.
> And what about the *group*?
> Did you even *think* about the group?
> I hope you know you've put me
> right in the middle of this mess.
> *Your* mess, Laren.
> Do you think I can take your side? Because I can*not*.

At some point during her tirade
the twisting and churning inside me stops.

I see the hopelessness of it and I

                                                let go.

This is not going to blow over.
Morgan is still yelling
when I power off my phone.

It isn't until mealtime that I fall a p a r t
Surrounded by mashed potatoes and peas,
baked fish and family
Mom, Dad, and Jackson.

That's when my throat tightens and tears fall.
Mom coaxes out some-not-all of the story as I circle
the facts and focus on the 'now-they-hate-me'
ending. Meanwhile Jackson feeds his fish to the dog.
But Dad
slides his chair around
and tugs me close
to his left side.

The countdown has begun.
I just don't know it yet.

The Shunning: Part One

There are rules
for what I've done. Specific punishments for
crimes against friendship.
I expect no leniency.

The first day will be the worst.
I've had time to prepare,
to imagine what's coming.

I'm ready.
Hard-as-stone ready.
They can bring it all—
the cold granite stares, disdain, disappointment.
I know what messages their faces will offer.
I know too
when they're certain I've taken in their silent fury,
they will turn away
ever so deliberately.
I've imagined it all and I've made up my mind.
There is no point in caring.

But my stomach is not ready.
It lurches when Nina storms by,
a little hallway tempest.
She spits out a single word as she passes.
And I remind myself that I will not care. I will not react.

I am halfway to class when I see Morgan.
I steel myself for more hostility, but it doesn't come.
Her eyes turn soft and sad. She looks miserable
as she lowers her gaze and moves past.
Her sorrow slams into me.
It was the one thing I wasn't prepared for.

It takes ten minutes in the toilet stall
to   pull   myself   together,
five more at the sink to get the red out of my eyes.
Now I need a hall pass

and some new friends.

Lunch

My eyes are trying to drift toward the table where my
friends, excuse me, *ex*-friends, are sitting.

I keep my head high, my gaze focused on the
elsewhere straight ahead,
which is how I manage to trip over a book-bag.
I don't fall
because it would have been a mercy
to have hit my head and knocked myself out,
 instead of lurching wildly and crashing
 into a couple of girls holding trays.

Let me just say that
it is not easy to look composed
under these circumstances.

Scott is with friends at their usual table.
I will him to look over and miraculously
 his head lifts and he see me there,
standing alone with my lunch tray
like the poster girl for friendlessness.
His hand comes up and I hurry toward him

ven though I am almost certain he was
waving, not beckoning.

So here I sit, pathetically soaking up the bits of attention that
dribble
     down
         during
breaks in the jock talk.

Every now and then
I see him remembering
Oh, yeah, Laren is here.
He smiles and makes an effort before
turning back to talk of games long over.
When he asks how my lunch is
for the second time
I am quite sure that
solitude would have been better.

But after school, he catches up, walks with me and
his attention is all mine.
As my hand rests warm and safe in his,
I have the oddest thought
that I am collecting moments.

Jackson

You are supposed to love your brother
because he *is* your brother,
but now and then he gives me other reasons,
like today, when I get home
and the little turniphead asks me if any of my friends
have smartened up yet.

Week Two

I'm making my dismal way toward Scott's table
where I've forced myself to eat lunch for the past week
because I've rid myself of options.

But then, I hear my name and I turn to see
Christine Oakey, who's in two of my classes.
She's sitting with a girl I don't know and
I'm not quite sure if she meant to invite me but I
barely hesitate before sliding into an empty seat.

Christine does a back and forth gesture between me
and the other girl. "Laren? Dee? You guys know each other?"
I'm about to say, "No," when Dee blurts,

> "I'm not sure if we ever actually met,
> if you know what I mean, but
> I've seen you around lots of times and
> I think we were both at a party at
> Paula-May Peterson's place one time, but
> in case you don't remember me, I'm Dee.
> It's short for Denise, but no one calls me that."

Dee prattles on and on. She hardly stops talking
long enough to catch
her breath, much less eat.
Maybe that's why she's so thin.
Christine and I finish our lunches while
Dee's chatter only allows her time for
          three tiny bites
of her wrap. I'm wondering if she's got an
eating disorder, when she
stops for breath,
glances down like she just noticed
she has food, and starts stuffing it in like a maniac.

Christine brings up the weekend in a vague
"you guys have any plans?" kind of way.
When I say that I'm not sure what
my boyfriend and I are doing
there's an awkward flicker of silence,
which makes me wonder
what stories Nina is spreading.

I want to say something,
give myself a kind of
casual absolution
but Dee has gulped down her lunch
and is jabbering again.
I half expect to see a wrap-sized lump
moving down her throat,
like a mouse that's been swallowed by a mamba.

Family (Anything But) Fun

My folks have planned a family bowling outing
this Saturday afternoon, which I think is a
misguided cheer-up-our-friendless-daughter thing,
	like going bowling with my parents and kid brother
	could ever be anything but depressing.

Except, that's apparently not the plan, since
Mom says I should invite
my young man.
(Yes, my mother is in a time warp. Thanks for asking.)
So they can get to know him.

As if I would ever ask Scott to do
anything that lame.

Answering the Call

It is NOT acceptable for ANYONE who is NOT ME
to answer MY phone
when I am in the shower.

And no, I am not overreacting or
making a big deal of nothing.
But it is hard to make a Mother Brain understand
just how serious I am about this
when a smile keeps sneaking onto my face.

Not a smile about what she did, obviously.
A smile that it was Scott calling and
it turns out he really likes bowling and
is coming with us this weekend.

But still. She had better not pull anything like that again.

The Shunning: Part Two

So.
My Facebook Friends list has shrunk by nearly forty.
Not your typical ebb and flow, but then
there is more at work here than
gravity.

*THERE ARE TWO SIDES TO EVERY STORY SO DON'T
JUDGE UNTIL YOU'VE HEARD BOTH OF THEM*

The caps in my status update are probably
overkill.
I leave them anyway.

A thought hits me, but it takes a little while
to find the courage to check.

According to Facebook,
I have no friends named Morgan.
I've gone from
Best Friend to Unfriend.
Discarded with a single click.

That feels a bit unreal. I try to push the hurt
out of my head and chest,
like I've been doing for weeks
but this time it's stubborn, like a
trick candle that keeps
re-lighting itself.

I picture them
Morgan, Angie, Nina
having the best time ever
while I watch people
                    seep
                        out
                            of
                                my
                                    life.

Unexpected Scott

Scott. At the door, smiling.
"Sorry for not calling first," he says.
His eyes are not sorry.
He is kissing me when
Jackson comes down the hall and makes
little brother barfing sounds. Scott laughs out loud and says,
"Hey, Jackson, how you doing? Put 'er there, man."
I can't help smiling as they do some kind of
secret guy handshake.

When I make coffee, Jackson swaggers in to
get himself a mug too and then sits with us,
trying to look like this isn't his
first cup ever.

It is ever so much easier to spot a
"first"
of something
than it is a
"last."

Phone Call – March 15

Mom has turned to stone,
except for her mouth,
which is moving without sound,
like someone has pressed pause on the remote
and the picture is fluttering ever so slightly.

When she hangs up she tells me to get Jackson
and get in the car.
There's been an accident.
It feels as though I am moving underwater,
the Unknown, a tidal wave of fear.

At the hospital, the emergency doors slide open.
We are sent down a hallway
> > > > > following yellow arrows.

Jackson runs into the room, gawking at Dad like
he's some kind of alien life form.
Mom bursts into tears and I
am not far behind because
the person in the bed seems
too small and frail to be my father.

We all say how glad we are that he's okay.
We ask if he needs anything.
Dad has a speech ready.

> This was a real wake-up call.
> It opened his eyes to what matters.
> He wants us to know that
> things are going to be different.
> We're going to be spending
> more time together
> from now on.
> No more late nights
> and weekends
> at work.

We can't stay long, because
he needs his rest. But before we go
his arms
open and when they close
I am inside them.
He promises that
everything will be all right.

We say goodbye and leave, defying the
< < < < < yellow arrows that guided us there.
There are no arrows to tell you how to get back to
where you were before.

After Accident

In the car Jackson announces that he's hungry.
"Can we have take-out, please, please, *please*?"
Mom agrees. "Why not? After all,
we have something to celebrate."

I call Scott when we get home.
He's watching a hockey game on TV.
I can hear it in the background, and also in
his voice as we talk.
"You aren't even listening," I say.
"It was scary."

Scott says, "Yeah, but you said he was okay, right?"
The announcer's voice rises in excitement.
I let him go back to the game.
There is no one else to talk to.
By 9:30 I'm in bed and asleep.

Second Call

The sounds tug me from sleep.
I try to crawl back into my dream but
they are coming
pounding down the hall
racing toward my room
slamming the door open.

My mother is in the doorway—
her face says everything even
before the words come
but they do come
those words.

I'm on my feet, ready to fight
because this is a lie, a *lie*, a LIE.
I'm on the floor, broken
because it is the truth.

Jackson is silent.
He stares from the doorway.
He stares ahead in the car.
I wonder if he could be sleepwalking.

A Minor Fatality

Arrows point you to the living but for
the dead you get an escort.
Mom tells the nurse that the injuries were minor.
The nurse answers that it's especially difficult when
it is so unexpected.

Everything is wrong:
the colour of his skin,
the way his face is sunk in,
as if the air is leaking out of him.

The nurse's voice is a meaningless
hum in the background. I hear random words:
driver, car, passenger, red light, seatbelt.
None of them mean a thing,
hovering behind us
as we try to grasp
what lies ahead.

As we leave, she tells us he didn't suffer.

Planning

At the kitchen table, Mom is
talking on and on. Making lists
as if she's organizing a party.
I am assigned to writing down names
as she blurts them out,
people we have to call with the news.

Jackson's foot swings against the table leg,
Thunk, thunk, thunk, thunk, thunk.
My brain sinks into the sound
until Mom runs out of words,
until her head drops and her shoulders heave.

That is when I notice that
the roots of her hair are gray.
She will need to colour them before the funeral.
I write this carefully at the bottom of my list.

Cinnamon Buns and other Edibles

I don't remember falling asleep.
My mouth is dry, my head aching but
the house smells good, spicy and warm.

Aunt Rita is here. She
calls me her *poor darling* and
tells me to come and have a cinnamon bun.
She has baked them fresh because
we all need to keep our strength up.

The cinnamon buns are huge.
I eat two while Aunt Rita fills me in on
what's coming. Apparently, it is not enough that
my father is dead.
I am also about to learn who my
real friends are. And
I might as well prepare myself because
even family members will let me down,
although heaven forbid that she should mention names.
I consider a third cinnamon bun but I already feel
like I might puke.

Mom appears in the hallway, her pain an invitation.
I'm on my feet in a flash,
racing to her,
grabbing hold.
Aunt Rita is held at bay
by the slippery mess of our faces.

By noon there is a steady stream of hands
thrusting food through the door.
Aunt Rita has a system for the offerings.
Casseroles and baked goods are sent to the freezer while
trays of veggies and plates of cold cuts
are stacked in the fridge.
Sorry about your tragedy. Have a snack.

The food-bringers talk to Mom, but
Aunt Rita answers most of the questions.
Everyone says what a shock it was, that
they couldn't believe it when they heard.
They hug Mom and take her hand. They say,
"Be sure to call if there's anything I can do.
Anything at all."
A few make her promise she will.
I watch them leave.
They look satisfied.

Grandma

Grandma Powell arrives at the same time that
Mrs. King lands with what she calls her
Famous Chicken Pot Pie.
She gives us heating directions depending on whether it's
frozen or thawed when we cook it. I hear a jumble of numbers
and the mention of tinfoil, which is when Grandma snaps.

"My daughter has just lost her husband," Grandma tells her.
"And these children have lost their father.
Do you think they want to hear
a lot of nonsense about heating up a pie?
Take the silly thing back home with you
if it needs that much coddling."

Mrs. King backs out the door clutching
her Famous Pie, staring at it in bewilderment,
baffled by the fact
that it's still in her hands.

Gathering Family

Memere and Pepere Olivier are on their way.
I think of Pepere peering over the steering wheel,
his back straight.
The image crushes in on me, squeezing my chest,
filling my eyes.

When they arrive
Memere crumples just inside the door.
Aunt Rita rushes her into a chair and bustles off
to make a pot of tea. Aunt Rita believes
tea is some kind of magic potion.
A solution for everything.
Got a tummy-ache? Tea.
Fight with your best friend? Tea.
Flunked your algebra test? Tea.

Death in the family? Tea.

Circle Talk

Memere does not understand how this terrible
thing could have happened, and
Pepere cannot believe that it is really true.
A day full of words
makes no difference at all.

When my brain cannot stand one more
minute
I escape to my room.
But something is wrong in there —
the air is thin and tight and
I cannot get enough of it into my lungs.
It is like trying to breathe
through my damp pillow.

The Wake

At the funeral home a tall, thin man passes out
pins that identify our relation to the   deceased.
We are given half an hour for a private visit with the   remains.
Everyone cries quietly, gathered around the   departed.

Morgan and her parents arrive soon after the doors open.
She hugs me and we cry and I
feel grief and hope and guilt.

So many people.
After a while it is as though we are stuck
in a soundbite loop.
Sorry for your loss.
Sorry about your troubles.
Such a tragedy.

Angie and Nina do not come.
That is fine. That is their choice.
But Scott also does not come and
my neck hurts from looking for him.

Funeral

I feel as though my father has been cheated.
There are prayers and hymns and readings but
no one gets up to talk about him:
what he was like and things he cared about.
Mom has decided against a eulogy and so
there are no humorous or touching stories.
This funeral could be for anybody and that
makes me angry because
it is the only funeral my father will ever have.

Panic surges through me when
the pallbearers walk down the aisle,
and the coffin carrying

My Father

is wheeled behind them.
I can hardly keep myself from yelling,
"Stop! There's been a mistake."
Jackson is trembling. I
yank him close to me.
He doesn't even struggle.

The graveside service is not like
they show on television. There is no lowering
the coffin into the ground, no handful of dirt or flowers
thrown on top of it. Even the hole is hidden
by a bright green cover.

Barely a Blip

The crowd is like a cloud
breaking up, drifting away,
returning to their own lives.

Only a few family members remain and
we gather at the table
eating, talking, even laughing,
just like everything is normal.
As if my father's death was nothing more than a
blip on the screen.

I think to myself that the worst is over
but that is because
I have no idea what lies ahead.

Comfort

Finally. A text from Scott.
He is so sorry. So, so sorry.
I want to ignore it, make him wait,
but the longing to see him is stronger
than my pride. I hate it when I am so weak.
It makes me feel pathetic but that doesn't stop me
from calling him.
He says, "Hello?" on the third ring. Not a single
word gets out before my tears begin. Finally, I sob,
"Please, can you meet me somewhere?
I feel so bad and I really need to see you."
Relief floods me when he tells me to meet
him at the tiny park on the corner of my street.
"I'm on my way," he says softly.

I see him walking toward me from the end of the block.
The rhythm of his steps brings a rush of yearning,
the urge to get up and run to him.
I hold myself back because I am
a tragic figure, huddled alone and
suffering on a bench,
and I don't want to spoil the image.

"I got here as fast as I could," Scott says.
He holds me close and
there is no seeking, no petition in his hands.
I press my face against his chest, inhaling
the scent of him and feeling
guilty about the warm pleasure it brings.
Until

the comfort of his touch, his nearness
gives way to sadness
gives way to pain
gives way to anger and
questions burn inside me.
I want to ask him, "*Why* didn't you
come to my father's wake or funeral?"
but the right moment is not there, or perhaps
something stands in its way.
I decide that is not the important thing.
I tell myself that what matters is that he came
when I asked him to.

Escape

Mom has taken a week off work so that she can
sort out our affairs. How do you rearrange
your whole life
in seven days?
Jackson and I turned down her suggestion that we
miss a few days of school.
It won't hurt, she says.
But she is wrong and all I want right now is
out.
The rooms are full of shadows and sighs.

School: Day One

Science class is just what I need.
Mr. Zallum's voice offers a resting place to my brain.
I sink into the low buzz, focusing on the
sound until I feel a jab on the shoulder.
The guy behind me is hissing for me to wake up.
Was I sleeping?
I'm not sure.
I turn slightly and nod my thanks because he
doesn't know what he took from me.

When the noon bell sounds I realize
I haven't written a single word all morning
though my history notebook boasts a couple of squiggly lines,
from when Ms. Ardena gave us our homework.
She's a hawk, sharp-eyed and ready to swoop down
on unsuspecting prey. The last thing I want is that kind,
or any kind of attention.

In the cafeteria I move slowly
as I pass the table where Morgan
and the others
are sitting. They stop talking and

look down.
I have entered a dead zone,
a pocket of silence surrounded by
a thrum of voices.

I keep moving. I try to trick myself into
believing I was not hoping for
an invitation.

I am sliding through the afternoon when
it strikes. A jolt, a flood.
I run out of class with words
pounding in my brain.
my father is dead
my father is dead
my father is dead

I am bent in half over the sink when
Christine Oakey comes in. She speaks quietly.
"I thought you might not want to be alone."
She's wrong. That is exactly what I want.
But the cool, wet paper towel she passes me
feels good pressed to my eyes.
"I need to go home," I say.
She nods and says she'll let our teacher know.

Problem

Mom is not at home.
The secretary is sympathetic but she cannot
let me leave the school without a parent's consent.
She tells me I can go to the sick room or the library.

I choose the library and wander aimlessly until
my attention is caught by a display of student work.

There, in the centre, is a book of stories and poems
published as a fundraising project.
Mom and Dad bought one for every
relative they could think of because
one of my poems is in there.
I take it down, and flip it open to 'my' page.

To Tristan from Isolde

by Laren Olivier

Where your thoughts wander, my love, my own
Away and away and away
Take me there with you, leave me not
For I am a child of the moon begot
Here in the dark, with the lamp forgot
Here with a song that the faeries brought
Here, but not bound to stay.

Where your steps wander, with dreams their guide
Hillside and rock and stream
Think mine beside you, quick and free
Farther and farther, yet held in me
And deep in your heart—where the shadows flee
For what shines within you will always be
As bright as the moon's own beam.

Where your heart wanders and finds its rest
Is the home that belongs to me,
For I dwell in safety within your hold
Trembling bravely, shy and bold
With a love that can try but can never be told
Captured on pages with ink gone cold
Steady and yours and free.

A memory that is still warm rises from the page:
Dad insisting that I read my poem aloud for the family.
When I finished they clapped and Mom
said it was very good. But Dad
didn't say anything. Not a word.
His eyes were misty as he put his hands
on my shoulders. He shook his head back and forth and
his face said *can you believe it*? as he
hugged me to him.

Glancing down now, I see several
wet and puckered circles
on the open pages.
I look at them curiously
as though someone else's sorrow has left these
wrinkled splotches on the
ill-fated lovers.

Home

Mom is working late,
catching up after her week off.
She says to order a pizza and use
Dad's bank card to pay.
She tells me the PIN number is 1027.
My birthday and Jackson's.

There is a glove around
my heart.
Squeezing.

A Different Delivery

One of Dad's co-workers is at the door,
dropping by, dropping off Dad's briefcase
so Mom won't need to pick it up.

Tucked inside the soft, worn leather of the case
is a small package. Something Ordered but as yet
Unopened. Mom's face is pale as she pulls out a
velvet box. Lifting the lid, her fingers tremble.

Mom says that my birthday is coming up. She says
This must have been a surprise planned for me.
The bracelet is beautiful and elegant and
unlike anything I have ever owned.

Here After

It bothers me when Jackson
has a question and I
don't have an answer.
Not just because I'm older
(and should obviously know more)
but because it is hard to face the disappointment
he can't quite hide.

That is why, when he asks, "Is there really a heaven, and
is our dad there?" I hate it that I have to say,
"I don't know." Which makes me
wonder why I don't, at the very least,
know what I believe.

Mom and Dad always said we could
make up our own minds when we were older.
That is not much help right now.

Every Cloud

Morgan is coming over!
And I know—I know that
this sounds
horrible, but
this is the one
good thing
that came out of
my father dying.

It is the strangest feeling
when joy and sorrow both
have claws on your heart.

Mixed Messages

Morgan is hardly through the door
when she tells me she
can only stay for an hour.
"I promised Mom I'd do something."

It is the "something" that hurts because it means
she couldn't even be bothered to
come up with a convincing lie.
Not that I want a lie from her. But,

when I raise an eyebrow,
a red cloud of anger floats
across her face. She knows me
well enough to see the accusation
in this small gesture.

We stare at each other, assessing
the rules that govern what we
can and cannot say
in the frame of this new beginning.

The clock slows as
we step around our words
and I have to admit that there is
a sense of relief
when she leaves.

I push away the disappointment.
We just need to give it more
time.

Comfort Zone

When I am with Scott there is a kind of
danger lurking in me, a reckless need to
wash away the pain.

It is with him that I find
places and moments where
tears and sadness are trespassers.
Places where
reality has floated
into the air and away
and every thought, every feeling
gives way to the travelling warmth of his touch.

That is when the blurring
begins, and I am glad that
my back is pressed against anything
that is not a wall.

Drama

It is Wednesday and I am making
my way through the cafeteria when
Tessa Landau hurls herself across
the length of several tables to
put herself in my path.

"I hope this won't freak you out," she says,
"but I think I was one of the last few people to
see your father alive."

I stare, which is all the encouragement
she needs. Her face puts on a display
of sadness and she says,
"I saw the accident. Your dad was
alive then. I heard he died on his
way to the hospital."

"You heard wrong," I tell her.
"My father died later.
From complications.
I was there."

I want to be sure that she knows
I saw him after she did.

"I'm glad you got to see him," Tessa says.
Then she adds, "And I'm glad your mom
wasn't hurt too badly."

"If you were really there," I say,
"you would know that my
mother wasn't even in the accident."

"Of course she was," Tessa insists.
"I saw her with my own eyes. I saw them
get her out of the car and put her
on a stretcher."

This careless lie disgusts me.
She is turning my father's
death into a bid for attention
I walk away because I am too
furious to trust my mouth.

Counselling

Someone-who-is-not-me
has decided I should be sent to the
private psychologist who books
appointments at the school one day a week.
So here I am, sitting through
Dr. Socorro's Psychological Sales Pitch.

 "A traumatic event, *blah, blah*
you may be feeling *blah, blah*
well-meaning friends,
cannot fully understand *blah, blah*
isolation, *blah*, death, *blah*, range of
thoughts and feelings."

My eyes trail around the room, lighting
without any real interest on
muted prints and paintings.

The brakes come on when I realize he is
repeating a question he has just asked.
"So, Laren, do you think that it would be
beneficial for us to meet once a week?"

My brain says, "Not even a little bit," but my
mouth goes, "I guess," before I can stop it.
It's kind of pathetic, how pleased he looks.

Lucky he doesn't read minds
or he'd know that while he
writes up my appointment card, I am
already planning my escape.

Looking In

I am horrid because
some days
I hate eating lunch
with Christine and Dee.
They are always
Perfectly Friendly. But I
am the Intruder.
An Outsider
who has been granted entrance to
a slightly foreign land.

Sometimes I watch their mouths move as
they talk or chew or smile. It is oddly like
watching a silent movie. That makes me wonder if
I'm going crazy. Maybe it won't be long before the
student eNews has its first interesting heading.
"Girl Suffers Psychotic Break while Eating Curly Fries!"

When the House Smells Good

I know before I see her.
Aunt Rita is here.
I know from the cooking smells
and lemony cleaning smells.
My sheets are changed,
the bathroom sink is shiny,
and at dinner we will not have to
try to think of things to say to
silence the terrible echo
of silence.

Lies in my Locker

I think it must have been Nina.
Yes, Nina. Who else would make up
something this mean and write it on a
piece of paper and stick it in my locker
like a coward?

*"Your father got in that accident because he was busy
with his hand up his girlfriend's skirt."*

Test

I walk slowly past the table where my
once-upon-a-time friends are eating
their lunch. I give them plenty of
time to betray themselves with
giggles and knowing looks. I
watch to see if they huddle
together in that certain way
that friends do when they are
gathered around a secret.

If the author of that terrible note is
among them, they somehow manage
to keep from giving it away.

I am not convinced.

Socorro

I forget my first appointment, so the office secretary
buzzes Mrs. Duthie's class to remind me.
I feel eyes following me as I
gather up my books and slink out.

Socorro's face lights up when he sees me. I bet
he's thinking how rewarding it will be to
haul me back from whatever ledge he thinks I'm on.
At least the chair is comfortable. I settle into it as

Socorro tells me I can discuss anything I want.
"It will be held in the strictest of confidence,
unless there's a crime involved, in which case
I have to report it," he tells me. "Although, I can
let you off with jaywalking or littering."
It isn't much of a joke but I award a smile for the effort.

When I ask what I should talk about
I am sure he will answer, "About your father's
death, of course. That is why we are here."

Except, he tells me, "You can talk about
anything you like."

It feels like I am picking my way along on
spongy ground. When I think about it later,
the only thing I can remember saying was that
a neighbour's dog has been barking at night,
making it hard to get to sleep.

Discarding Dad

Mom has thrown out or given away most of my father's things.
She boxed it all up and sent it to Goodwill or
wherever it is that you send dead people's clothes.

Jackson got Dad's watch and it was like it didn't even matter
if he took care of it. The next day he had it on
in the backyard when he was goofing around
with one of his friends.
I yelled at him to
take it off but Mom said to
leave him alone. She said it was his
and he could do whatever he liked with it.

It serves him right that it went
missing later that day.

A Visit from Morgan

Did you know that there is a
way of smiling
that says, as loud
as a shout,
"I do not
really
want to be
here."

Locked Out

Jackson is sitting on the front step when I
get home from school today.
He is sitting there because the door is
locked.

When I join him, he gets up and
begins pacing
back and forth
back and forth
back and forth
across the driveway,
which is irritating until
I realize that he is
watching for Mom
and he is
afraid.

I want to promise him that
she will come, that
nothing will happen to her, but
the words won't come.

When Mom finally shows up I
give her a helping of the
open, honest feelings she is
always asking for. And she says,
"I am too tired to fight with you today, Laren."

Like objecting to being
locked out of my own house
is unreasonable.

Under Glass

Later, there is a gift.
Not a peace offering or an apology token.
A real gift, planned and prepared for reasons
unrelated to a locked door.

Mom taps at my door. She enters looking
nervous. Her hand clutches a frame, picture side
away from me. She clears her throat and sits
on the bed next to me before
placing it gently into my hands.

I am expecting to see my Dad's face
but my eyes find
both of us,
a summer vacation moment
captured
when I was thirteen.

Mom and her telephoto lens had
found us in a canoe on the river.
We are paddling toward shore and although we
are not smiling, our faces are full of joy.

I cannot tear my eyes away from it.
I want to tell Mom how perfect it is
but all I can squeeze out of my throat is,
"Thanks."

Her hand lights like a butterfly on
my arm. She smiles as she
slips out of my room.

Like all of her smiles lately, it
contradicts itself.

I could tell you that my father
saved my life that summer
but I won't because I don't know for sure
whether I would have drowned if
he hadn't been there.

Mom had told us a dozen times:
Whatever you do, stay close to shore
but I decided she only meant Jackson.
I was old enough to look after myself. Until,
that is, the shore slid farther and farther away and
the tide started an argument that it seemed likely to win.

Panic was closing its fingers around my chest when
I heard my name and saw my father,
running toward the water.
Then I knew I was safe.

Two other memories cling to that one.
The way he clasped me to him. And
Mom scolding that I had put us both at risk.
But that was not true. *He* put *himself*
at risk. To save me.

Curious Companions

I have begun to think of them as
The Opposites—my new lunch-mates.
Dee, the scattered, frenetic chatterer
and Christine, quiet, serene and steady.

That makes me wonder what invisible forces
are at play, creating friendships that
should not work.
But do.

It's an idea I never gave much thought
before because I always *knew* why
I was friends with Morgan
and Angie and
Nina.

Ducky Scott

I'm walking with Scott by the pond in Elmwood Park, when
a mother duck and her parade of fluffy young
waddle past and slip into the pond like
they're entering on a water slide.

Surrounded by her babies, Mom begins to
quack and Scott insists that she is
bragging about her kids.

He drops to the ground, lying flat,
(*on her level*, he says) and then
he quacks back at her, all the while,
translating their "conversation" for me.

I join him, flooded with joy, with laughter,
until there is no room for
anything else.

Socorro

You'd think a head doctor would give you some
advice, but all I get are questions. They
sneak up on me, like some kind of
pop-up therapy. Today, he starts off with,
"Can you tell me why you think you're here?"

"Because my father died?" I say. And even though
I am sure that is the right answer, he waits. Silently.
I am certain that this is something he learned in
Psychology School. It must be one of the ways patients
are tricked into revealing things they would rather
keep to themselves.

"I am not going to talk about my father," I tell him after I think
he has waited long enough. "Not to a stranger. It's too
personal."

"That is always your choice," he tells me.

Sadness Schedule

Ms. Ardena's arms are crossed over her chest.
"We have been more than patient with you,"
she says. "Now the time has come for you
to get back on track."

I sound like a derailed train, which might not
be all that far off. I wonder,
but am not foolish enough to ask,
if she is speaking for all of my teachers.

Apparently, there is a limit to how much
slack I can expect to be cut, and that limit
has been reached. By my calculations, the
magic number is seventeen school days.

Food Fight

Jackson has decided
to become a vegetarian and
Mom has decided
that he will eat what she tells him to eat.

"No way am I going to start cooking
separate meals for you, buster," she says.
"I have enough on my plate as it is."
(Which, I alone find funny.)

I wonder where this idea came from
or how it is that our own mother seems
oblivious to how stubborn Jackson can be
when he's pushed.

Finding a Voice

He might deserve some of the
credit so I have decided to tell
Socorro about the idea I got at
our last session. Writing has
always been the one thing that
works for me. It is an outlet, a
sort of blood-letting, only what
I am letting out isn't blood. Or
maybe it is.

It begins with a poem that finds its way
to the shredder because even when I am
emotional I can recognize melodrama
when I see it. Next there are rambling
thoughts and words and feelings, none
of which anchor themselves to anything.
I am about to give up when, at last, my
words find the form they need.

Letter to Dad.docx

Dear Dad,

How strange is it for me to be writing a letter to you when you are never going to read it? Maybe I really do need to be seeing a psychologist—which I'm actually doing. Can you believe that? To be honest, it's not as bad as I expected. For one thing, this letter I'm beginning today is because of something he said. He told me I should find a creative outlet—a way to put pain outside of myself where I can look at it later on.

There have been a lot of bad days since you died. Not whole days—I wouldn't want you to think we're all falling apart—I know you'd hate that—but moments that sneak in and stop you in your tracks, if you know what I mean. Like yesterday, I was heating up a can of soup and I remembered the time you made me laugh so hard that I spit soup clear across the table. (Kind of poetic justice that it hit your shirt, don't you think?)

That got me laughing, but then it turned into tears, which happens a lot. I didn't expect happy memories to make me so sad. Mom says that will change in time. She says that someday we'll be able to remember the good things without them turning on us.

Right now, the one thing I really want to tell you is this: I miss you every day.

Sinking In

Fooling yourself is pointless—
did you know that?
You start out feeling optimistic about
something and you want to stay that way.
You want it so much that you will
invent all kinds of excuses to keep on
believing.

But let me tell you,
when you run out of lies and hope,
the crash is harder, more bitter
because you have been party
to your own deception.

And, just for the record,
Facebook is right.
I have no friends named
Morgan.

Wrong Numbers

Two hours have
just been spent
thinking of replacements
for the gaps in my
phone contact list.

Even with Christine and Dee added,
the damage Nina did left
a lot of holes.

I can't believe My Ten
now includes
grandparents.

Passenger

This is not because of the stupid,
anonymous
note in my locker,
but I am
wondering.

I am remembering
the nurse at the hospital
mentioning a passenger.
And, I have realized that Tessa
believed what she was saying,
even though she was wrong when
she said my mother was in the
accident with my father.

That must mean that someone was with
my father when the accident happened.
A co-worker, perhaps, or someone
who needed a drive.
And whoever it was, she may be able to
tell us about his last day.

Those final details of
his life do not
have to be
lost
to
us.

Conversation with Mom

When I tell Mom that I believe there was
a passenger in the car with Dad that day
she doesn't look surprised.
She doesn't look curious.
She doesn't look at me.

I stand there while the clock
patiently, relentlessly, counts out
seconds and ice forms inside me.
When my mother speaks,
it is only to say, "I am tired, Laren.
And I do not want to have
this conversation."

Truth

I am not a child.
I know things.
I know about life and betrayal.
Lies and cheating have put down
solid roots, even by my age.

But there are things that are possible
and things that are not possible,
and this is not possible.
Not by my father.
Not to my family.

I pull the impossibility of it to me
wanting it to undo the awfulness that
stares me in the face.
It is a struggle I am terrified I will lose.
Which is what happens when what cannot be
crashes into what is.

Best-Friendless

I want to call my best friend.
I want to talk and listen and
laugh and cry. That is always
how it works, reliable as the
sunrise. We could drink cocoa
with tiny marshmallows and
lie out under the stars and feel
the universe roll over our troubles.

Because that is what you can do
if you are not best-friendless.

Rita

Aunt Rita is one of those people who
knows everybody else's business. A gossip,
news-bag, rumourmonger. She will chase down
a scandal or dig through
the ruins of someone's life until she gets hold of
the juiciest bit of news she can scavenge.

I begin to watch her. And because I am paying attention
I see things. I see
that she knows about the mystery
passenger in my father's car that day. I also see
that she is not sure whether or not
my mother knows. I could
tell her but I am a shadow.
I am eyes and ears with a
breaking heart.

Scott's Perspective

According to Scott I should forget
about this whole business because
there is nothing I can do anyway.

According to Scott nobody is
perfect and you've got to take
the good with the bad.

According to Scott what I need is
to go for a good run around the track.
Apparently, that will clear my head.

Wondering

What was she like—IF (and I am not
one hundred percent convinced)
there really was another woman?
Younger and prettier than my mother?
I hate the thought of that. Worse is the
idea that it could have happened because he was
having a midlife crisis of some sort.
Like a pathetic token in a game of cliché.

I try to think of a reason that's big enough to
explain it. A reason that isn't
common and cheap.

Letter to Dad.docx (continued)

There have been some pretty big changes since I started this letter. I almost feel like going back and erasing the first part, but my psychologist said I should keep everything. No matter what. Anyway, I've got some things to say to you. First of all, you can't even begin to imagine how furious I am. Because I know—I know you were NOT ALONE in the car that day.

And just in case you care, I'm not the only one who knows. Mom does too. Remember Mom? Your wife? The woman you married and promised to love until death do you part? Looks like you blew that one, didn't you? It makes me sick when I think of the way you used to talk about values and keeping your word. Oh, and honour! What a laugh. What a load of rot. What a liar.

I wonder what excuses you made up. Did you decide you were having some kind of midlife-thing? Was it that pathetic and common? Buying a red convertible would have been better if that's what it was. At least if you went off and killed yourself driving some super-fast car, people would have less to gossip about.

And it wouldn't hurt quite as much.

Nina Speaks

There are some things you never say to anyone
no matter what they've done
or you *think* they've done.
Nina finds such words today.
They land in my chest with
a weight that I cannot
carry by myself.

And Christine says,
"She is just angry. She did not
really mean it."
So, I say, "I know."

As if choosing to believe something
makes it true.

Picture This

I used to love to watch Mitch Hedberg on YouTube,
laughing even though I knew the punch lines.
Like, when he talks about a friend who said to him,
"Here's a picture of me when I was younger."
And Mitch says,
"*Every* picture of you is when you
were younger."

I like Mitch's brand of comedy
(which he took from us for one last high)
but today I've been browsing
my picture files and
that particular line has turned
sad and heavy.

All of my photos are
an earlier version of my world.
The faces that are there,
over and over. Pictures of
Morgan and Angie and Nina.

And my father. They're like the
Before Side of the story of my life.
It strikes me that the
After Side is empty—
there's not a single picture
of my life now.

I am
emptied of so much.

I try not to think about the losses—
the ones I couldn't prevent and
the ones I could.

Movie

Scott likes:
war movies
action movies and
comedies, unless
they're chick flicks.
I can live with that.

So we're at the theatre,
in the centre of
the back row,
watching car chases
and shootings,
sharing a gigantic
bag of popcorn and
a bucket of root beer,
which I like almost
as much as orange Crush.

The Jackson Assignment

Mom can't take any more of Jackson's
foolishness. Or so she says.
Would I *please* talk to him?
She has tried until she's blue in the face.
"I am worried sick that if he doesn't
eat soon, there will be nothing left of him."

I tell her that vanishing vegetarians are not a
big problem in our society.

And she says, "If you think you are being cute or
helpful, Laren, you are very badly mistaken."

No problem.
I have been wrong before.

The Jackson Assignment: Part Two

It's startling to see how
neat Jackson's room has become. I
don't mention that when I ask if I can come in.
"I want to know more about this vegetarian thing," I lie.

His eyes narrow, which tells me he suspects I was
put up to this, but he starts talking anyway.
His face is small and serious and he counts on his
fingers, reciting his reasons.

Pinkie: His friend Brad's family is now vegetarian.
Ring: The food is healthy, even though he doesn't like the taste
of some of it.
Middle: Brad's mom says meat is gross.
Index: Brad's mom says we should not eat other living
creatures.
Thumb: Brad's father's cholesterol is getting better.

There are no fingers left when he tells me that he tries not to
think about Burger King too much.

Mom corners me the second I emerge.
"Did you talk to Jackson?" she asks, like maybe
I just went in there and took a nap or something.

I open my mouth to tell her about his
reasons, but what I actually say is,
"It's fine. You should
leave him alone."

Dee Takes a Breath

Sometimes, Dee's lunchtime orations
can seem oddly restful.
Like rain on a metal roof, the words just
keep pouring out of her, *ratatatatat, pliplipliplip,*
until I'm suddenly aware of my
unawareness.

I think she might have a future as a hypnotist
or sleep therapist. But today, out of nowhere,
mid sentence—a sudden silence.

Christine and I both stop chewing and
turn to her, on alert. Which is when
Dee asks, ever so softly,
Are you doing okay, Laren?

Friday Night

This was a lousy week but it's over now and Scott
is taking me to a concert. Some local bands
in the park, warming up for summer.

Mom does her best to kill the mood.
"Where are you two going?
Is there going to be any drinking?
What time will you be back?
Do you have your phone with you?
Is it charged?"

Then her Mother Brain recites the exact words I hear
every time I'm going somewhere with a guy.
"Call me if you need me. I don't care what's
going on or how late it is."

Once we've escaped, Scott gets me laughing,
mimicking Mom.
"Why won't you kiss me?
Do you like to see me suffer?
Don't you know I'm crazy about you?"

I'm still giggling when he stops and pulls me tight
against him. His kiss is long and slow and his
voice is a soft moan when he tells me that he
likes me—so much. I want to answer, but I
can't speak. All I can do is grab
this moment's perfection, and place it ever so
carefully on memory's shelf.

We take our time, walking toward the park,
watching the sun
slide into a golden pool,
and the world, with its night breeze and early summer
flowers, swells with the beating of my heart.

Too soon we are there. Too soon the magic
is jostled and crushed by the feet and faces of
the crowd.

Year-End Report

How did I not see this coming?
I knew my grades were slipping, but not
like this! This is a disaster. A free fall.
I barely made it through.

Meanwhile, Jackson's grades have actually
improved, which makes him eager to
show Mom his report. That prompts her to ask
about mine, which I'd hoped she
might not think of until
it was misplaced somewhere.
Like in a shredder.

I brace myself for the big freak-out. As expected,
her eyebrows shoot up, then come together in a frown.
But when she looks at me, there's no anger. No
yelling, no hands on hips—nothing.

Instead, she lets out a small, sad sigh and says she
understands and she knows I'll get back
on track in the fall and in the meantime
I shouldn't beat myself up.

It is like I've moved to an alternate universe.

Socorro

Socorro's notepad is in hand, as usual, while
some manic version of myself has
taken over my mouth.
I can't help but wonder what he might be recording
from today's rave.
Patient's brother dislikes eggplant?
As I try to think of a new subject, Socorro wonders aloud
if something about Jackson's vegetarianism is bothering me.

"Not exactly. It's just—
He's never shown the slightest interest
in healthy eating before."

It startles me to realize that Jackson must *have*
a reason—one of his own, that wasn't
supplied by Brad's mom. Why haven't I seen that
or tried to find out what it is?
I wonder if that reflects badly
on me as an older sister.
I change the subject.

Drifting Days

I love the gentleness of early summer.
The warm breezes.
Walks in the evening's
whispering dusk.

Food Fight: Part Two

Mommie Dearest has a new strategy to
force meat down Jackson's throat.
She's decided to starve him into
submission.

At dinner, she plunks steaks
on the table.
Nothing else.
I'm surprised the salt and pepper shakers
are still there.

She sits down to eat, acting like it's
perfectly normal. Like we've *ever* had a
meal of nothing but meat.

Jackson stares ahead with his
chin up until Mom looks ready
to crack, but all she does is tell him,
"You can leave the table if you
aren't going to eat your dinner."

As soon as I can, I smuggle a peanut butter
sandwich to his room. His door opens the
second I tap on it.
That tells me he
was waiting,
which means he
knew I would come. And for
some reason this
breaks my heart a little.

Disappearing Familiar

Some kind of makeover frenzy has taken hold
of my mother. It started slow—a new
hairstyle, acrylic nails, a gym membership and some
wardrobe additions that, if you ask me, are
not quite right for someone her age.

That was fine. But her new obsession is
taking over the house. Everywhere you
look there are stacks of home-decorating magazines with
colour-coded Post-it notes in cryptic messages.
A hieroglyphics professor couldn't crack
Mom's codes. LvC W ov BMCr: H b X C
She corners me at least once a day and
forces me to invent an opinion, which depends
more on my mood than anything else. It's not
like I could care a whole lot less—

except, that is, about my parents' room.
Her room now and she has changed
everything. My father wouldn't know
where he was if he walked in there today.

Scott

He insists that he is not
insisting, but I feel the
change, the way he
presses me.

I tell him *wait* because
I do not want to say *no*
even if *no* is what I am
thinking.

And when he asks me
what I am waiting for
I do not seem to know
the answer.

I only know there is one.

Aunt Rita and Grandma "Help"

Grandma and Aunt Rita remind me of chickens
pecking away at each other non-stop.
Peck, peck, peck. Pick, pick, pick.
I don't even think they notice
what they're saying
half the time.

Today is different. Today they have
hatched a plan to talk Mom into
signing up for a painting class.
With *them*, no less.

They lay out their persuasions.
Anyone can learn to paint.
It will be a hoot and, most of all,
Mom *spends too much time cooped up.*

Mom clearly doesn't think their idea
is all that it's cracked up to be.
She tells them thanks but no thanks.
Painting doesn't interest her and
with work and errands and whatnot,
she gets out more than enough.

I am surprised when they give up without
an argument, although Grandma does
look a little like she has had
her feathers ruffled.

Suspicions

The voices in the back of my brain will not stop,
hinting, probing, whispering words that
cannot be true and do not belong.

I hate them because I know they
are false—must be false and yet
they will not leave no matter
how many times I
tell them to go.

Socorro

I say, "I am writing a letter but I do not want to
talk about it and I still do not want to talk about my father."
To which he says, "Why do you think that is?"

I could tell him that it hurts when I think of
past things that are gone forever, or
future things that will never happen, but he
must know that.

I wonder, though, if he knows that the greatest
pain is in the smallest details and it is the
details that I do not
want to examine.

Where we were going or why has long since faded
in memory. It is that place in the road that I recall,
the place where our attention was caught by
several men gathered around a fear-frozen
young deer. They pushed and tugged until
the frightened animal took a few halting
steps and then began to move,
jumping forward toward the ditch.

Joy filled me. A crystal clear moment at the thought that
these kind men had stopped to help
a creature of beauty
to safety.

But then, a terrible sound shattered the air.
The sharp crack of a shotgun and the truth
penetrated my heart. The hands I thought were
helping were instruments of death—
driving the deer from the road
so that they could shoot it.

I sobbed so hard that my father pulled our car
to the side of the road, where he came around to
my side and knelt in the gravel
circling me with his arms. He listened while
I said appalling things about what I hoped
would happen to those men.

Dream

Last night I dreamed that I had fallen
from a great height.
Down, down, in a plunge
toward a dark and terrible
place filled with
nothing.

I reached to grasp a rope,
dangling there,
but each touch
of my hand
made it unravel
until my only hope
was a single
frayed
strand
that
could
never
hold
me.

Jackson's Fat Lip

Jackson comes home from a Friday night at Grandma's with
his lip split and swollen to about twice the normal size.

He heads straight for his room while Grandma tells us
how he started a fight with a boy on her street. Mom yells,
"Jackson, you get back out here right now."
His shoulders slump more with
every step toward the table.

She fires questions at him, the kind that have
no answers, and quite frankly
I don't see the point of the interrogation since
she already got the whole story from Grandma.
I know he's not going to answer but
I wish I knew why he did it.
Jackson never gets in fights.
He likes everyone.

Letter to Dad.docx (continued)

Dr. Socorro says that we have built-in defences that can block things until we're ready to deal with them. That must be why my brain changes the subject every time I think about The Passenger in your car that day.

Scott says I should give you the benefit of the doubt. But I don't know how much doubt I even have, considering Mom's reaction.

All I know right now is that I don't want every thought I have of my father to be about That. I'm still adjusting to you being gone. That feels like about all I can handle right now.

Do you remember last year when Mom moved the clock that used to be over the kitchen sink? I must have glanced at the empty space it left behind hundreds of times.

Well, not to compare you to a clock, but it's a bit like that. I keep "glancing toward you" and finding an empty space over and over again.

Even when life seems normal, it isn't. I miss you. So much.

Empty Days

This is the
most horrible
summer of my life.

First of all,
Scott is gone   away
with his family for
the whole month of July.
A month long holiday.
Who does that?

Meanwhile, I'm stuck in the house,
babysitting Jackson. When he's home
that is. Sometimes he's at
his friend Brad's place. I picture them
sitting around eating chunks of
tofu with lentils and beans and
waiting eagerly for the after-effects.

Even with that, I can't helping thinking that
Jackson's life is more exciting than mine.

Friendless

Christine and Dee seem to have
disappeared, which is a bit strange.
Not that we got all that close, but to go from
eating lunch together, chatting on
the phone and even hanging out
a couple of times, to
a whole lot of
silence ...
I can't help but
wonder what happened.

I try to sound casual on the phone
when I ask Christine why
I haven't heard from her lately. Somehow
it comes out like an accusation.

There is silence before she asks,
"But when did *you* ever call me, Laren? I
wanted us to be friends, only
sometimes I felt
more like a stalker."

I have no answer. What she said is true.
That will be that, I guess. I am about to
end the call when she adds, "Dee and I are
going to a movie tomorrow afternoon.
Do you want to
join us?"

Standing My Ground

I'm ready and waiting when
Mom comes through the door.
It is about time she found out that
I am not
a built-in babysitter.
I am going
to a movie with Christine and Dee
tomorrow, if it means
Jackson has
to stay by himself.

Rehearsed words are in my head but anger
pushes them out of order and they fly
out of my mouth and into the air
like stray bullets.

I brace myself because I know Mom will say,
"I am not in the mood for this, Laren.
You are not asked to do much around here.
I do not like your attitude."

Instead, hugs and
promises turn my
anger to
tears.
It is a strange,
guilt-filled
victory.

Show Time

By the time the coming attractions begin to play
I've learned that Dee finds Zac Ephron and
Robert Pattinson super hot, but that if she
had her pick, she'd go for Chance Crawford.
This elicits an inside joke from Christine,
which makes both of them laugh and reminds me that
I am still an Outsider.

I try not to think about Morgan and Angie and even
Nina. I tell myself that I am here at a movie with my
new friends, even though I don't believe it, and then

as the show begins, a scene makes us laugh and
something shifts ever so slightly.
A tiny shard of warmth makes its way into me.

Socorro

I let Socorro know how much I want to be there
by flopping into a chair and answering his
annoyingly pleasant greeting with a grunt.

"You seem unhappy," he observes.
"Amazing diagnosis," I say. "That must be
why you make the big bucks."

He counters with silence
an impassive face,
out-waiting me.
Classic Socorro.

"It's summer," I grumble.
"You might find it hard to believe but
sometimes I have better things to do
than sit here and talk about nothing."

"I see," he says with his shrink voice.
"In that case, please feel free to switch or even
cancel now and then. My summer schedule is quite
flexible and I want our sessions to benefit you."

Now I feel foolish because there were no big plans
but I am still glad I told him how I felt. Finding out I
have options changes everything. Sometimes,
it's just about having a choice.

Dinner at Christine's

I make it halfway through my first meal at
Christine's place before I start wondering how
soon I can leave. Mrs. Oakey is a great
cook but she is also a believer in
interrogating her dinner guests.

"You poor child. How *are* you holding up?
And your poor mother, is she managing all right?
It must be such a difficult adjustment for you and your
poor, dear brother, with your father passing so suddenly."

What is she expecting? Does she imagine that I might
get up on a chair and give a heartfelt speech
at dinner? To *strangers*?

Afterward, (no dessert, thank you, I really could not
swallow one more bite)
I follow Christine to her room,
wondering why she didn't warn me.
She manages to blurt out, "Sorry!" before
collapsing on her bed, laughing so hard she can hardly
catch her breath. This annoys me until

she gets herself
under control and launches into a
hilarious imitation of
her mother, which, for some reason she
delivers in an Irish accent.

"Aw, you *poor, pathetic* creature!
Is your heart so broken you can barely chew your food?
Surely you'd like to tell us all about your
innermost thoughts and feelings!
Pay no mind to the fact that
we only just met you
four minutes ago."

The next hour is a blur of laughter
and girl talk.

Long Distance Scott

I have to say that texting
back-and-forth is less than
satisfying and anyway,
how many times can you
text someone that you
miss them like crazy?

Hey! You up yet?	Ya
Anything interesting going on today?	No
Sounds familiar :)	Lol
At least you have a beach there, right?	Ya
I love beaches. Building sandcastles,	
and collecting shells and stuff	Cuz your a girl
I thought you liked that about me ;)	Haha
I sure miss you	Me 2
Well I guess I should get going	K
Bye for now	By

Being apart sucks.

Neighbourhoods

The streets give rhythm to my
impatience, beating out thoughts of
Scott's return, a few more days,
a few more days, a few more days.
And what began as an aimless walk
moves me with its own purpose until
I find myself surprised, or not surprised
at all, at the corner of Morgan's street.

I can see her house from here. It is
a measurable distance, like the space between
then and now, from the place where we
were friends to this point where we are
something not yet defined. It is a longer
and shorter time
than I can grasp.

I now know that I did not, could not,
would not believe
this chasm could open between us.
It did not seem real when she was there—
in the hallways and classes and lunchroom.

When at any second she could have
looked my way and smiled and said,
"Hey, Laren."
When normal was possible and I could
still see a way back.

So I stand where my empty heart and
longing have brought me. A journey that
pride will not let me complete.
And I turn away.

I'm downtown, stopped before a window display of
stained-glass lamp shades, when a man and his
small daughter emerge from the store. Her face is
grumpy and sleepy, but when he scoops her up, her
little fists fly at his chest and she
hollers that she can walk *all by herself.*

Time shifts and another scene unfolds:
one where *I* am the
little girl.

The child I was
in this moment from my long ago
has gaps where teeth have been
and this makes the me-in-memory about
seven. My class had just returned
from a day-long excursion, a bus ride that
began noisily, song-fully, joyfully, and ended
with zombie children, sluggish and cranky.

There's a hazy recollection of feeling stiff and out of sorts, as if
I'd just emerged from a cozy snooze, although I don't
believe I'd actually been asleep. I recall the
bright light of the sun in my eyes as I took that
last big step down off the bus.

And then my father was there, lifting me up, but my hands
shot out and I shoved myself away from his hold.
"Don't!"
I have no idea what made me react
that way. I only know it wounded him.
In this memory, that is the only detail that is clear.

Letter to Dad.doc (continued)

I was getting some earrings out earlier when the birthday bracelet from you caught my eye and I slipped it on my wrist. Mom calls it the gift you sent me from the great beyond. And maybe it is. But an uglier possibility occurred to me while I stared at it.

Maybe it wasn't meant for me at all. Maybe it was for her. The Passenger.

I'll never know for sure, will I? Oh, I'll wear it, and I'll try to tell myself that it's a final gift from my father. But part of me will always feel a bit like a thief.

Funny thing—the first thought I had when I put it on was that I should write a note thanking you for it. So, thanks. I guess.

Dee's big Splash

I can hardly believe my ears when Dee says,
"So, bring him with you,"
because she's talking about that dreaded
creature, the-nuisance-no-one-wants-around—
the little brother.

They have an amazing in-ground pool
and with the sun blazing, her initial invitation
seemed almost cruel as I explained that I am
stuck home today, with Jackson.

But Dee is unconcerned with the thought of
a nine-year-old tagging along.
"He'll have fun," she says.
"The more the merrier."

I watch her laughing as he beats her at a game
of water Frisbee. I smile as he trails along
behind her to fetch lemonade and snacks.
I think to myself: he adores her.

Socorro

I'm in my weekly meeting with Socorro when
something inside me snaps. It's odd because I
wasn't at some cathartic moment. It comes from
nowhere, a tidal wave of words,
rushing, crashing, tumbling over each other
on their way out.

"It's so hard trying to sort through everything," I say,
putting away my tears. "I don't know what it means to me.
How *can* I? I didn't know what it meant when it was
happening. I didn't even know it *was* happening. I thought
my father was something he wasn't."

"What is it that you thought your father was,
that he was not?"

"That should be *obvious*," I say.
"I thought he was a
good person, a good father.
I thought his family was
important to him, that he
loved us more than anything.

Me and Jackson and Mom.
But if he was having
an affair, that means
none of those things are true."

"Does it?"

I make my voice sound like I am explaining
this to a small child.
"Of *course* it does.
What else *could* it mean?"

His eyes are still as he
waits for me to answer
my own question.

The Return of Scott

I had not expected, when I
opened the door to find him there,
that he would seem more a stranger
than my boyfriend.

It is as if the month away has made him stronger,
more commanding. Joy clashes crazily with
a curious unease and my stomach quivers
in confusion. His mouth hurries to mine.

I will myself to find the thrill.
He is so close. So close.
The room tilts. Scott murmurs
something, a smudge of words
that I do not need to hear
to understand.

I am thankful that Jackson
is home.

Back-to-Normal Jackson

Scott is here so instead of the usual
lazy lunch, I make grilled cheese and bacon
sandwiches with cold, sliced tomatoes,
dill pickles and potato chips.
Jackson watches Scott gobble his
sandwich and says he will have
bacon, too, the next time.

At suppertime Jackson puts a
single fish stick
on his plate with his fries.
Mom, for once, has the sense
not to mention it. We eat in silence until
Jackson breaks it with an announcement.
"Guess what! I'm not a vegetarian anymore."
Just like that.

Mother-Daughter Day

I humour her because she has enough
on her mind and anyway it won't
kill me to spend a day out
with Mom. Besides, I
could use some new
clothes for school.

By noon there are shimmering heat waves
rising from the pavement and I am more than ready
for a break even though I'm a little worried about lunch.
It has crossed my mind that Mom might be planning
a heart-to-heart, "how are you *really* doing?" kind of talk
and today is one of my hollow days.
I'd like to keep it that way.

I'm dipping a chicken ball into sweet-and-sour sauce when
she reaches across the table and puts her hand on mine.
I wait, dreading what's coming, but all she says is that she
loves me and Jackson more than anything in the world.
And then she cries.

The Real Thing

I love Scott.

We are sitting at the table in his kitchen, eating hotdogs when
I notice a little blob of ketchup at the corner of his mouth. It
bobs up and down as he chews. So I reach over with a
napkin and dab it, and he turns and smiles and looks
into my eyes for a second longer than he needs to.

And it hits me.
It crashes into me.
I love him.
I *love* him.

I can't finish my lunch.
I tell him I'm full.
I *am* full.

School and Other Miseries

I swear that August melted under the blazing sun,
soaked into the ground and drained away.
Its bright new promise a yellow swell,
a golden trance, while the moon
conspired to distract us with
thirty-one lazy winks.

I can hardly stand the thought of early mornings,
trying to focus on boring subjects
dragging home stupid assignments
hearing the Mother Brain Rules for school nights
and worst of all is that Dad isn't even
here to negotiate.

What?
I wonder if could I even *be* a more horrible,
selfish person. My father is
dead and my big regret is that he
can't make things easier for me anymore?

Except, that isn't what I mean.
It's just one more gaping hole in the fabric of my life.
A hole that cannot be mended or hidden. There is
no way to un-rip something.

Socorro

My new math teacher looks at me
warily when I pass her the slip
that allows me to leave class for my
weekly appointment with Socorro.

I tell him, "You should have seen her
face. I swear that she thinks I'm crazy
or something." And, of course, he
asks, "How did that make you feel?"

I think that over and then tell him,
with a smile, "You know what? It kind
of amused me, but it also gave me a
strange sense of power."

There is a kind of freedom in
having this
one place in the world
where I can say
anything I
want to.

I like how he never tells me what
I should think or how I should feel.
I know he's guiding me
with his questions but
it is always a path to
my own solution.

Letter to Dad.docx (continued)

Remember the chats we used to have about school—the ones I tried to avoid? Well, this would have been a good time for one. Since classes went back in, a lot of the people who were snubbing me have come back around. And, to my surprise, it hasn't meant much to me. In a way, I actually feel a little embarrassed for them.

It's different when it comes to Morgan. That's been hard, and it's felt hopeless for a long time. Until this afternoon, on my way to french class.

I was heading toward the language department when I saw her coming down the hall toward me. For months she's been acting like I don't exist so I was startled to see her looking straight at me as she got closer. We were almost face-to-face when she offered a sad smile. And I swear I heard her whisper, "Hi," as she passed. So, I got wondering whether I should give her a call or send her a text or something. It seems likely that she was giving me an opening because she wants to fix things between us. But what if I'm wrong? Or what if it was a trick?

Trying to figure out what to do made my head hurt. And then it hit me—I don't have to do anything. I let go and, just like that, all the troubling thoughts and questions floated away.

Sometimes it's a lot easier to just wait and see what happens. That seems to be my new philosophy. I've turned into Miss Inertia.

Four-Tier Cake

You never know when something will
slam into you. Like today, at my cousin's wedding.

I hate weddings. You expect them to be romantic but
what they mostly are is boring. You wait
for pictures, you wait
for dinner, you wait
for speeches to be over, you wait
for it to be late enough that
you can leave without being rude.

Jackson is seated on my left. Dad's watch,
too big for his wrist,
sits halfway up his arm. There was a near breakdown
over it earlier. He ran about wailing that
he *needed* to wear Dad's watch and
he just *had* to figure out where it went.
Luckily, I was able to "find" it. (Also lucky was
how no one found that suspicious.)
I don't think he will be careless again.

At our table, Grandma and Aunt Rita are
vying for that coveted title of The Person with the
Sorest Feet. Grandma's corns and bunions take us
through the salad but Aunt Rita gives her a run for
her money during the main course, when she
parades out her swollen and strap-strangled tootsies.
There is still no clear winner by the time our
half-melted gelato arrives.

The deejay's voice takes over the room, inviting
the newlyweds to the floor for their first dance as
husband and wife. They gaze at each other like
they are still posing for pictures, which,
I suppose they are.

I see a wet shine on Mom's cheek.
No doubt she is thinking back to
her own wedding day, while the
Father-Daughter dance takes me
forward to mine.

It is a new, raw moment of loss,
knowing there will be no dance with
my father at *my* wedding. He will not
walk me down the aisle or lift the veil
away to kiss my cheek before
I turn to face my groom.

As I struggle not to cry a small arm reaches
across my shoulder and I feel Jackson's
head lean toward me. Sometimes I just
want to grab that kid and squeeze.

And then, a memory.
Theirs, not mine.
About me. And my father.

I was five (Grandma says six) and my
dress was yellow (Grandma says orange)
with a white sash. Everyone agrees I was
adorable and the story presses forward.

The scene is set with lights and tulle
at nuptials from some yesteryear.
A handsome chap bows deep and asks
if he can have this dance with
His Best Girl.

I'm told I giggled,
suddenly shy, as I was
led to the dance floor and
twirled about in
my father's arms.

Slowly, slowly,
an image forms and becomes
the ghost of a memory.
I will invite it to
grow and bloom until it is
fully formed,
so that someday,
the day it is needed,
I can take it out.

The Truth about Veggies

Jackson's friend is coming for dinner and
Jackson doesn't want Brad to know that
Jackson is back to wolfing down meat, so —
Jackson asks Mom to serve veggies and say nothing.

It sounds harmless to me, but Mom
gives him this big lecture about
being open and honest and not
trying to hide things.

As if we haven't spent the last eight months
in the shadow of my father's lies,
like ghosts, pretending to be real people.

Losing Face(book)

Facebook or not, I doubt I would ever have seen
that picture if it wasn't for Nina. I know she was
behind the tagging, making sure it got to me.
Making sure I
had that image burned into my brain.

A picture of my boyfriend
Scott
with his arm slung around a girl-who-isn't-me.
Someone named Samantha.

I should have called him the second
my insides unfroze but
I did not. Instead, I
sent him a copy of the picture
with no message, which I
expect he got loud and clear.

When he calls to tell me they were
joking around, it was nothing, I
reach out to wrap myself in
his denials because

it is only fair to give him the benefit of the doubt. But I am on high alert now. No one is going to make a fool of *me*.

That's for sure.

Like Mother, Like Daughter

My thoughts have turned to my
mother and I cannot help but
wonder. Were there signs?
Did she suspect? Maybe there were
clues and hints and she
refused to see them.

I wish she did not feel that
she has to close me out. I
am almost a woman. And
I am part of this whether she
sees that or not.

A Visit to Aunt Rita

Time alone with Aunt Rita makes me uneasy.
She plays the confidante like a pro, drawing
words out of me like a hypnotist.

I learned this lesson for the first time when I was ten and
had my first crush. Making cookies in her kitchen,
I told her every silly thing while she
smiled and nodded,
understood and allowed.
In those moments I felt that I loved her
more than anyone else in the world.

And then she betrayed me, exposing my secret with
words and winks, playing the innocent while
I burned with shame and fury.

I have no more secrets for her and it
satisfies me to know this will always
be true. Today, I go seeking, and she
does not know that she has taught me
well or that this time her secret
will be spilled into my hands.

It is easy, so easy, when someone wants,
longs to tell. And now I have the name.
Doris Menrick.
The passenger in my father's car.
The Other Woman.

A Random Thought on Solitude

When I was little I thought hermits
(much like goblins and faeries) only lived
in story books. Then I heard about
Gold MacEvoy, a real live hermit who went
deep into the woods on the north side of town
after a broken romance, and has been there
ever since. Rumour says he started out
panning for gold (which explains the nickname)
but liked the solitude enough to stay.

It is easy to think that anyone who went off
to live away from the rest of the world must be
more than a little odd. But there are days lately
when I am not so sure.

Socorro

I joke that if only I had known
I could have had my sentence reduced
to half time, I would have made myself
talk about The Issues
from day one.

There is a quick smile and then, the usual
serious face. "That would have slowed
your progress more than taking
your time did," he says.

But he is pleased with me. Because I am
facing what needs to be faced.
I am pleased as well,
and not just
because I now only
have to see him
every second week.

My Father's Birthday

Memere and Pepere are here for the first time since the
funeral. Summer came and went with phone
calls and excuses, instead of their usual visit.
But now they are here, to honour
my father's birthday, even though Mom
pointed out the drawbacks of a late fall visit.

Memere tells us she has been asking God to help
her understand why, but so far God has not
revealed the answer. Pepere gets choked up telling
a story about my dad when he was a little boy.
Which makes the rest of us cry, too.

Mom has turned stiff and ill-at-ease
as if she is spending the day
in the company of strangers.

I see her relief when Memere and Pepere
go out after lunch, but when
they return with a birthday cake
Mom grasps a chair and sinks into it.

Memere, blissfully oblivious,
opens a package
of candles.

My eyes are drawn back to it
again and
again
throughout the meal. Perhaps my brain
is convinced that one of these glances will
find it is no longer there, was never there,
that fluffy white frosting and cheery blue trim.
I chew and swallow, chew and
swallow, chew and swallow.

Mom flees to the kitchen with the dinner plates,
when Memere brings the cake
to the table. The cellophane lid crackles as
Jackson stares and Mom becomes a
mannequin beside the sink.

Memere lights the candles, telling us, "Now
we will sing, so that Marcel will know
he is not forgotten."
Her lip trembles as she speaks.
When all of the candles have been
crowned with flames, Memere clasps
her hands before her chest as though she is
praying. She lifts her chin and begins to
sing in a high, quivering voice.

Happy Birthday first, then *Bonne Fête:*
a celebration of a birthday that
will never be. When the bizarre performance
is finally over, Memere
cuts the cake.
We eat in silence.

Farewell

We have gathered in the doorway.
Goodbye! Goodbye! Smiles and waves
follow Memere and Pepere as they
back out of the driveway and begin
their homeward journey. No one speaks
as the little blue car disappears
around a corner. This is not
an event for words.

The cake, or what   remains
of it, disappears shortly
after they have   departed.

Christine, Queen of Calm

I like how Christine spreads
her quiet words and ways
over anger and upset.

She has that rare ability to
smooth and soften
just by being.

She is the last person I expect to
tell me to *stop putting
things off.*

She is also the first one
who does.

A Call to Doris Menrick

She is right, Christine. My new friend.
There is not always
a right moment. Sometimes,
waiting for it to
arrive is just a way of hiding. So, this moment,
right or wrong, will be the one.
I make the call while carefully planned words desert me.

"I want to know the truth," I tell her.
"It wasn't the way you think," she says.
She begins to cry. Sobs wrench themselves from her.
I hope she drowns in her own tears.
She says, "Your father was a good man."

"I know what my father was," I say.
"I do not need
you, of all people,
to tell me that."

I have found the one truth I need.

Halls

Most of the time, I never notice the
sounds in the school hallways.
But there are days when
noise bounces and crashes
off the walls like thunder. It clings to
my brain. It echoes on and on.

I imagine being able to silence it:
the gossip and secrets and lies
all muted.

Confronting Scott

The Facebook picture is a festering sore that will
never heal. I cannot stop myself from
clawing at it.

It does not help that I feel an
absence in him today, even though
we are on his couch, making out. A little.

When I ask, "Who are you thinking about?"
it hangs in the space between us while he
puts on a parade of emotions.
He offers me insulted, amused, indignant —
and I know that they are nothing more than
faces he is trying out.

Anger is his last resort, as though he can
bully me into
believing him.
"You sound like *Nina*," he says, and I
can no longer turn away
from the truth.

I *should* sound like Nina.
I have taken her place.
It is time to stop
pretending, to stop
deceiving myself.
I remind myself that it was
innocent, that nothing really
happened, but I was there. I know
the way he stared into my eyes while she was
at his side. There were signals and messages as clear
as words, and they were sent
from two sides of the table.

Confronting Me

I tell myself that I must find the truth, but I do
not think I will get it and I am unsure whether
an admission or a denial will hurt me more.

The thought comes
that I should break up with Scott.
I push it away.
I have sacrificed for this guy,
given up friends, faced social scorn.
He *has* to be worth the choices I made.
I cannot let myself think anything else is true.

At home later, I crawl into bed, completely exhausted.
The night is dark outside my window—dark and
lovely with white, glittering stars.
Lucky stars, far, far away.

Socorro

It is near the end of today's session when Socorro
tells me he doesn't think I need to see him anymore.
When I realize he means it (as if he might have
become a big jokester overnight) I cannot find
anything to say. He waits, as he always does, and I
summon a lame joke about how I will miss
the comfortable chair. There is a
faint smile before he tells me I have
done really well and that I can
make an appointment any time
I think I need one.

All these months I've been complaining about
these appointments, and now it
hits me that I really haven't minded. It's been
good to have a safe place to talk.

I leave with an odd feeling of sadness and
something unidentified
but good.

Chick Flick

Drowsiness is slipping its arms around me, which I hope
will go unnoticed. Christine and I are at Dee's place watching
"The Notebook" but my eyes have grown so very, very heavy.
If I could close them, even for a moment or two
without anyone noticing
and lobbing popcorn at me—

Dee's arm thumps into my side but she is not trying
to wake me. "I *love* Ferris Wheels," she proclaims,
breathless as the big ride turns on the screen.
And a memory nudges me as surely as her
elbow has just done.

I am at my father side, waiting proudly in
line for my very first ride on the Ferris Wheel.
I glance at Jackson's stroller where he sits
blue and sticky with cotton candy and
my happiness lets me pity him.
Poor little guy, missing out.

A worker clicks a metal bar in place, tugs it for
good measure, and we begin to rise. But something is
wrong. It is not magical, wonderful, thrilling,
the way I have imagined.
It is horrifying and frightening and
I am sure I will vomit all over myself because I am
too afraid to lean forward.

The horror holds me firmly until an arm
folds me against my father's chest and his
voice reaches through my terror.
"You're okay. I've got you. Just close
your eyes and breathe slow and deep. In and out and
in and out and in and out. You're doing great."

I remember the circus smells that day, drifting
blending, beckoning. Hot dogs and fried onions.
Popcorn and ice cream and candy. Even the grease and
metal of the rides. But best of all was the
scent of a freshly ironed shirt.

Wounding Mom, Wounding Me

They come out of nowhere. No, that is
not true. They come out of anger,
out of pain, out of some black and
evil place where Self is all. Words
I can never take back, sent out to attack
in a fight I cannot even remember.

"No wonder Dad had a girlfriend."

Strange
how they turn back to stab at me.
Before she begins to speak, I am already
condemned.

"Is that what you really think, Laren? *Is* it?
Because the truth is, you don't know
anything about it. Nothing.
Whatever your father did
or didn't do, was *his* choice.
I will not be accused or
blamed or held responsible
for his actions."

I think she is finished but before I can
slink away, she adds, "And just so you
know, I do not intend to discuss this with
you or anyone else.
Not now and not ever."

Sooner than Never

Even though she said, "Not ever," she comes
to me only hours later.
She comes with an announcement.
There is one thing she wants to say.
One thing she wants me to know.
I wait in silence while she struggles for
composure. When she speaks, her
words sit still in the air.
"This does not have to affect you, Laren.
If he was running around, it was on *me*."

It amazes me how little she
understands. Does she really think I can
go along when everything I've known and
believed and trusted
about my father
has crumbled into dust?

Letter to Dad.docx (continued)

Sometimes I feel so bad for Mom. She's doing her best, even with all the things she never had to handle before, but it's not easy for her. Like, last week—she got ripped off by some guy who was supposed to clean out the gutters. He asked for half the money up front, supposedly for materials, and then he never showed up. Jackson tried to persuade her to let him do it, if you can imagine.

Jackson says he's the man of the house now. I feel like the only one without a new role. Maybe that's because I haven't quite let go. Sometimes a thought forms of something I want to tell you, or I look toward your chair with a split second expectation that you will be there. That hurts, but the thing that bothers me the most is that we don't feel like a real family anymore.

Jackson's Microwave Emergency

A tap at my door.
Jackson's pale face.

"I broke the microwave."
His voice trembles although
I can see him fighting it.
"I forgot to take off the
tinfoil. Then there was
a flash and sparks and it
caught on fire."

"Don't worry," I tell him but
it takes more than words to
convince him that he has not
added one more thing for
Mom to carry. When I have
proven to him that all is well
his relief almost makes me
cry.

Truth and Lies

I have made my way at last to the truth
about that girl. Samantha (as if her name matters).
It has been inside me the whole time,
chewing its way to the surface.

Now that looking forward and
looking back have collided,
I know, I know, I know,
what I did.
What I *really* did.
I knew it then.
Meeting his eyes with whispers
in mine. So much was said that never
saw words.

Was there a millisecond when I
truly believed it was just a
game? Harmless flirting,
a delicious thrill
that meant nothing.

I have been carrying the proof all this time,
and now it is my own voice that
mocks and condemns.

I must act before I weaken,
before I tell myself more lies and try
to pretend that I believe them.
I will betray myself
if given the slightest chance.

I do my best to explain to him
that it's been doomed from the start,
that you can't build something good on a
foundation of betrayal and deceit.
Our beginning makes it impossible for me to
ever feel safe.
And my heart is breaking.

He says, "Okay, if that's
what you gotta do," and
I close my phone, slowly, like I am
making a statement, but
Scott has already hung up.

How casually he has let me go.
Which is good because a part
of me knows how easily
I could have been persuaded.

They are Here

They are here—
Christine and Dee.
They have come
because I need them.

They are here—
armed and ready.
They have come
to fight my pain.

They are here—
with ice cream and words.
They have come
with a message.

They are here—
to say it will be all right.
They have come
and they are here.

Letter to Dad.docx (continued)

Something happened today that brought back a powerful memory. It started when I found Jackson at the table, staring glumly at stacks of magazines. Of course, I asked him what they were for.

"An art project," he said.

"The project you were all excited about a couple of weeks ago?" I asked. "The one you said was going to be amazing?"

"Yeah," he admitted. Then his eyes lifted and he gave me a mournful look. "It's due tomorrow."

Naturally. "What were you planning to do?" I asked.

"The Scream."

"That doesn't exactly clear it up for me."

"Have you seen that painting called The Scream—by Edvard Munch?" When I nodded, he went on. "I was going to make that out of cut up magazine pictures. Like a collage."

Can you believe it! A collage of The Scream! I knew it was hopeless even if I worked on it with him until midnight. Then I remembered—when you have friends, you can call on them.

And I have friends.

Christine and Dee both said they'd help and in no time, they were here, brandishing scissors and craft glue and smiles. They told Jackson it would be fantastic and gave him buckets of attention that he soaked up like a sponge.

Dee had printed out a copy of The Scream and she did a pencil sketch of it—complete with colour coding instructions—on Jackson's Bristol board. Then we all flipped through magazines, tearing out pictures and cutting up sections of colour.

As he was sticking the colours into place, the smell of the glue reached me across the table. In an instant, I was transported across years, into my grade two classroom. The image that came to mind was crystal clear—a folded piece of purple construction paper that I was painstakingly cutting into the shape of the bottom of a shoe. I was working with greater care than usual because the task at hand was a card I was making. For Father's Day. A sole-shaped card with my goofy school picture inside and the caption. "Upon my sole, I love you DAD!"

I remember the way you scooped me up in a bear hug and told me it was wonderful—the best card you'd ever received. That made me giggle.

For a second, I think, "That was a great acting job, Dad!"

But right away, I know I'm wrong. As impossible as it seems, I realize that you really and truly found that lame card wonderful.

BTW. You'll be glad to know that Jackson's project turned out fantastic. He could hardly wait to show it to Mom when she got home, and a thrill ran through me when I saw how the sight of it picked her up.

It was a good day.

Truth and Consequences

You think something is over, a closed book, and
then something will pop into your head.
Today, it was a curious question.
Did Samantha know about me? Not
that it much mattered from
this side of the vacation.

Either way, what I did was so much worse.
It feels so strange knowing that I was guilty of
something so despicable.
And for what? For
someone who showed me on
Day One that he was a cheat.

And so was I.
Does that mean I
can never be trusted?
I can't stand to think I have
that kind of character flaw.
I will accept only that
there was a terrible
crack in judgement.

Today
and every
tomorrow
I will be
my own sentry.
I will not be
my father's daughter.

Mother the Invisible

I don't know exactly what grabbed my attention, my
heart. Mom is on the couch, laundry basket at her side, a
growing pile of folded clothes on the coffee table.
Justin Hines is playing in the background and she is
singing along to 'April on the Ground.' Her face is not quite
sad, but solemn, and somehow vacant.
As though there is nothing there. As if
she has taken up residence in a trance.

I realize that this is how she has looked for some time. She is
here, doing what needs to be done
    going to work
    coming home
    taking care of things
but there is a flatness behind it all.
She has always been serious, but there was
laughter there too. There was ...
interest. There was light.

I wonder about the way she threw herself into
redecorating the house, remaking herself. There was
something frantic about it, as though it was merely a way
for her to propel herself through the days. And now,

she lives in a state of autopilot.

I cross the room to her side, reach into the
laundry basket for something to fold. She gives me
a thin smile. I tell myself I should put an arm around her, but
I can't reach across the space.

She glances at me with a vacant smile.
Her hands go on folding clothes. I am
startled when she begins to speak.

> "I've been thinking lately about the summer we
> went camping.
> You were five and Jackson was a baby. I didn't
> work so money was tight. We borrowed
> a tent and sleeping bags—your dad loved camping,
> though I can't say the same about me.
>
> "One night we were sitting
> outside the tent, enjoying the cooling breeze
> after a hot day—
> watching the moon's reflection on the water. It was
> beautiful and peaceful
> at first until the mosquitoes drove us back inside.
> I made a remark that it would have been perfect
> if it wasn't for the mosquitoes. And your father said,
> 'Nothing is ever perfect,
> but that shouldn't stop us from taking hold of
> all the good there is.'"

The space between us closes.

Moving Past Scott

Of course I've seen him with her—
his new girlfriend, Meredith. She's
a clinger, the sort who hangs off her
boyfriend's arm like she's attached with Velcro.

There's a sad twinge, now and then, I won't
deny that's there. But I've seen more than
the two of them together. I've seen his
smile cross the space to her friend.

It is possible I am reading more into that
than I should. But I doubt it.

Forgiveness on Demand

I have been told that Nina is ready to forgive but
I know she was dragged to this place.
I know that the others chipped away,
chipped away at her anger and
determination, that they muffled her
objections with persuasions.
And with promises that were
not theirs to make. That is because they
believe it can be repaired, this broken
circle of friends.

I know it cannot. Not the way they
imagine. Good as new. Not after a wound
so deep, so carelessly inflicted. And
the casting off was too complete.

Yes, I could go to Nina today.
I could say my part and she
could say hers, but the truth
would leave our words
exposed and naked.
It would be nothing more than
an act in two play-ers.

ACT I, SCENE ONE

LAREN
    (imploringly, crossing hands over chest)
    Oh, Nina, I'm so sorry.
NINA
    (slowly lifting tear-stained face)
    I forgive you, Laren.
    (Hallelujah chorus plays in background.)
    (fade to reality)

The truth is, I *am* sorry.
I am disgusted by what I
did. But even with that, there is a
a looking-out-for-me side too.

I know I have made a start.
I have walked toward sorry
but she has steps to take as well
and healing cannot begin until
she walks toward forgiveness.

I hope for a measure of reconciliation
somewhere on the path ahead but we have
not reached that place.

Some things are heavy to carry
and yet
you cannot set them down just anywhere.

Bridget Jones's Men

I step from the shower to the sound of
voices down the hall. Mom and Aunt Rita
talking about the men in Bridget Jones's life.
Specifically, their personal preferences.
I stand there, dripping and amused, until
I hear Mom declare that, "Firth is hotter."
That is the point when I step into my room
laughing out loud, struck by how much
they sound like teenage girls.

It is funny until later when I am texting
Christine about it and she texts back:
"I guess your mom will start
dating one of these days."

New Year

What do they really mean,
these dark, winter, midnight bells?
An ending? A beginning?
Reflections and resolutions—all at the
passing of a single day.
Time.

It moves around,
my sense of time.
It is yesterday.
It is forever,
and each new occasion is a fatherless first.

My thoughts turn to him and to
the unfinished letter.

I open it and read what has come before,
leaving it all just as it was written. Even those
things that I would not write today
had their time and place, and will remain.
My fingers pause, poised over the keyboard
and then new words come.

Letter to Dad.docx (conclusion)

A lot has happened since the moment when Mom stood in my bedroom doorway and said the words that changed everything.

I've been angry with you. But lately, I've been angry with myself, too. I've been learning that forgiving my own mistakes isn't that simple, even though I'm truly sorry for what I did. I think you probably know all about that. You might have had some advice for me if you were still around. Or, you might not.

Of course, anger has only been a small part of it. These have been the most emotional months of my life. So much of it left me worn out, lost and empty.

Then, as I thought about the past year and all that's changed, I found myself sorting through some specific moments and memories. Nine in all. And something still settled in me as I realized that each of these had one thing in common. You know what that was? Your hugs. I saw that, through all of the bad and sad and glad moments, my father's arms were there to protect or comfort or celebrate with me.

Tears come when I remember the hug you gave me on the night you died. It was "goodbye" although we did not know it. But like every hug you've ever given me, it was also, "I love you. I'll always love you."

And now, looking back and seeing past the moments to the

whole, I know I can forgive you. That I will forgive you. It may take a while longer, but I've already begun.

I'm just now beginning to feel ... ready.

For what lies ahead.

With love from your daughter,
Laren